An I Can Read Book®

The Smallest Cow in the World

KATHERINE PATERSON

pictures by

JANE CLARK BROWN

SCHOLASTIC INC.
New York   Toronto   London   Auckland   Sydney
Mexico City   New Delhi   Hong Kong   Buenos Aires

I Can Read Book® is a registered trademark of HarperCollins Publishers Inc. All Rights Reserved.

All rights reserved. Published by Scholastic Inc., 557 Broadway, New York, NY 10012, by arrangement with HarperCollins Publishers. SCHOLASTIC and associated logos are trademarks and/or registered trademarks of Scholastic Inc.

ISBN 0-439-45502-2

12 11 10 9 8 7 6 5 4 3 2 1   3 4 5 6 7 8/0

Printed in the U.S.A.

To all the children of the
Vermont Migrant Education Program
K.P. and J.C.B.

Marvin Gates lived with his father
and his mother and his sister May
on Brock's Dairy Farm.

On his farm, Mr. Brock had two dogs,

eight cats, and ninety-seven cows.

One of the ninety-seven cows

was named Rosie.

Rosie was the meanest cow

in the world.

She butted the big dog.

She switched May's face.

She stepped on Dad's foot.

She pushed Mr. Brock

against the barn wall.

Nobody liked Rosie.

Except Marvin.

"I love Rosie," he said.

"She is the most beautiful cow
in the world."

"Ha!" May said.

"You don't feed her.

You don't wash her.

You don't milk her.

You don't shovel her manure.

10

She doesn't butt you.

She doesn't switch you.

She doesn't step on your foot.

She doesn't push you

against the barn wall.

You don't know anything
about Rosie."

"Yes, I do," said Marvin.

"I know Rosie is mad because
Mr. Brock took away her calf."

"You are the dumbest boy
in the world," May said.

"Mr. Brock always takes the calves."

That spring Mr. Brock said,

"I am going to sell Rosie."

"That's good," May said.

But she was wrong.

"I am getting too old to farm,"

Mr. Brock said.

"I am going to sell everything

and move to a sunny place."

Marvin's father was sad.

He had to find a new job.

Marvin's mother was sad.

She had to leave her garden.

17

May was sad.

She had to leave her school
and all her friends.

But no one was as sad as Marvin.

"Rosie is gone," he cried.

Dad gave Marvin a hug.

Mom gave Marvin a kiss.

But Marvin did not stop crying.

"Don't cry for Rosie," May said.

"She is the meanest cow

in the world."

Marvin cried louder than ever.

Soon the Gates family moved.

Dad worked hard on his new job.

Mom planted a new garden.

22

May found a new friend named Jenny.

Everyone was happy.

Except Marvin.

"Marvin needs a pet," said Mom.

"Do you want a kitten?"

"No," said Marvin.

"I want Rosie."

"Do you want a truck?" Dad asked.

"No," said Marvin.

"I want Rosie."

"Don't be a crybaby," May said.

"There are

one hundred and twenty-one cows

on this farm.

Find yourself another cow."

"I don't want another cow,"

said Marvin.

"I want Rosie."

"Too bad," May said.

"You will never see Rosie again."

Marvin looked at May.

He stopped crying.

"That's good," May said.

But she was wrong.

The next day

Dad looked at the trailer.

It was covered with scribbling.

Mom looked at her new garden.

All the flowers were pulled up.

May looked at her books.

They were all over the floor.

Everyone went to look for Marvin.

Dad was worried.

Mom was worried.

May was mad. Very, very mad.

"Marvin!" she yelled.

"I am going to get you!"

33

Marvin was sitting in the field.

He was smiling.

"Don't be mad at me," he said.

"I didn't do anything. Rosie did it."

"Rosie?"

"Yes," he said.

"Marvin," said May,

"you are the dumbest boy

in the world.

Mr. Brock sold Rosie.

She is far, far away!"

"Stop!" Marvin yelled.

"You nearly stepped on Rosie."

He pointed at the grass.

"There's nothing there," May said.

"There's Rosie," said Marvin.

"She came back! And she got small."

"How do you know it is Rosie?"

Mom asked.

"She is black and white,"

said Marvin.

"Oh," said Dad.

"And," said Marvin,

"she is the meanest cow

in the world."

"I thought Rosie was

the most beautiful cow

in the world," said May.

"She used to be," Marvin said.

"Now she is the meanest."

"Oh," Mom said. "What happened?"

"She didn't want to move,"
said Marvin.

"It's no fun to move.

And she doesn't like being little.

It's no fun being little."

"But how did Rosie get so small?"

asked Dad.

"Her new owner was a witch,"

said Marvin.

"Rosie did not like her.

Rosie butted her.

Rosie switched her face.

Rosie stepped on her foot.

Rosie pushed her

against the barn wall.

The witch got mad.

She turned Rosie

into the smallest cow in the world."

"Well," Mom said, "I think
Rosie needs a barn of her own."
"You are right," said Marvin.
"Someone might step on her."
"Or she might pull up
more flowers," said Mom.

"She might draw on more walls,"
said Dad.

"She might tear more books,"
said May.

"Yes," said Marvin.

"She is very mean."

Dad got a little brown bottle.

He poked some holes in the lid.

"Here," he said.

"Here's a nice dry barn for Rosie."

"Rosie likes her new home,"

said Marvin.

"She will not be mean anymore."

Marvin was happy at last.

"That's good," May said.

But she was wrong.

Marvin played with Rosie all summer.

He talked to her.

He fed her grass.

He milked her.

He took Rosie everywhere,

even to bed.

"Marvin," Mom said,

"school begins next week.

You will be very busy there.

Why don't you leave Rosie with me?"

"I can't," said Marvin.

"Rosie wants to go to school.

She wants to be the smartest cow

in the world."

"Oh," said Dad.

"Oh," said Mom.

"Uh-oh," said May.

Marvin took Rosie to school.

All the other kids laughed at him.

They laughed at May, too.

"There is the girl

with the crazy little brother,"

a boy said.

"Do you have a cow

in your pocket, too?" a girl asked.

"Moo!" said another girl.

"Moo! Moo!" said another boy.

May did not know what to say,

but her new friend Jenny did.

"You kids are dumb!" Jenny said.

"You don't have any imagination.

Marvin has a great imagination."

Jenny gave May an idea.

After school May said,

"Marvin!

I have been looking at Rosie.

She can't go to school anymore."

"But she wants to," said Marvin.

"She wants to get smart fast."

"She will have to wait," May said.

"Rosie is going to have a calf."

Marvin peeped into Rosie's barn.

"You are right," he said.

He was smiling.

Then he looked sad.

"Will anyone take Rosie's calf
away from her?" he asked.

"No," Mom said.

"Rosie and her calf

will live together always."

"But Rosie can't go to school now,"
said Marvin.

"That's OK," Dad said.
"She knows how to take care
of her calf better than anyone."

"Will you always like Rosie?"

Marvin asked May.

"Of course I will," May said.

"I think she is

the most beautiful cow in the world."

"We all love Rosie," said Mom,

and she gave him a kiss.

"Will we take her with us

if we have to move to another farm?"

asked Marvin.

"We will never leave her behind,"

said Dad, and he gave Marvin a hug.

May said,

"No matter how small she is

or where she lives

or if she's smart or dumb,

Rosie will have

Dad and Mom

and you and me

and the smallest calf in the world.

She will never be lonely again."

"That's good," said Marvin.

And he was right.